*This first edition
is published in simultaneous cloth and paper bindings,
with one hundred special cloth copies
numbered 1-100 and signed
by the author
and twelve hors commerce copies
lettered A-L and signed
by the author.*

AVAILABLE FROM FULL COURT PRESS

Collected Poems. Edwin Denby.
I Remember. Joe Brainard.
First Blues: Rags, Ballads & Harmonium Songs, 1971–74. Allen Ginsberg.
The Luis Armed Story. Tom Veitch.
Selected Plays. Frank O'Hara.
I'll Be Seeing You: Poems 1962-76. Larry Fagin.

Rebound Series:

Where I Hang My Hat. Dick Gallup.
The Frank O'Hara Award Books:
Spring in this World of Poor Mutts. Joe Ceravolo.
Highway to the Sky. Michael Brownstein.
North. Tony Towle.
Motor Disturbance. Kenward Elmslie.
Domes. John Koethe.

ALSO BY LARRY FAGIN

Parade of the Caterpillars
Brain Damage
Two Serious Poems and One Other (with Bill Berkson)
Twelve Poems
Landscape
The World of Leon (with Ron Padgett, Michael Brownstein, Bill Berkson)
Rhymes of a Jerk
Seven Poems
Poems Larry Fagin/Drawings Richard Tuttle
Potboilers

LARRY FAGIN was born in 1937 in New York City. He grew up in Los Angeles, lived and traveled in Europe through the 1950s, and received a B.A. degree from the University of Maryland in 1960. He moved to San Francisco in 1962, becoming part of the circle of poets around the late Jack Spicer. He lived in England for two years and, in 1967, returned to New York where he edited *Adventures in Poetry* magazine and pamphlets and served as a director of the Poetry Project at St. Mark's Church. He conducted writing workshops at the Brooklyn Children's Museum and has continued to teach creative writing to children in public schools. Currently, he directs Danspace, the dance program at St. Mark's, and is on the faculty of Naropa Institute in Boulder, Colorado.

and I sit here
in my dressing gown
read my telegrams
and count my blessings:
I have a few books
a few records
$78
a few pieces of furniture
a couple of pictures
a little dope
and a good girl
with a healthy body
and a sound mind
to keep me from going insane.
I just hope that's enough.

*

Dear friends
if this reads
a little heavy
it is because
I feel
a little heavy now.
I wish you all
health
wealth
and happiness
and with these
my last words
I fall back
onto my pillow.

LAST POEM

There are no words I understand
and I view this life
in a rear-view mirror
clamped onto the head
of my penis.
I can't make any sense out of it.
I see before me a bowl of grapes.
Now the grapes are gone.
I ate them all
but still it makes no sense.
I walk over to your house
ring the bell
you open the door
you say come in
and it's ridiculous
and I feel silly.
I feel stupid
and you look silly
and I feel certain
that the world is nothing
but a big booger
God picked
out of his massive concrete nose.
When I think of this
I go crazy.
What's the point of living
on a piece of snot?

*

But sometimes I think the star
is on my door

Until the whole screen bubbles

With tiny heads

Pink green mauve white

As the figure of

A blue skirted girl is split

Into four

Refracted

Again and again

As in the splintered image of a kaleidoscope

Amber and gold

Snow drop and clover leaf

The color in its wacky patterns

Achieves something of the intensity

Described by Huxley

Under mescalin

Finally the cast emerges

From the center of the kaleidoscope

Singing

"A Journey to a Star"

Wears a metal sleeve

Electrically illuminated

Which dissolves into a succession of

Metal hoops

Glowing brilliantly

As they wind away into

A pitch dark screen

Accompanied by a sumptuous and exotic

Arrangement for strings

Girls

In mauve leotards

Swing the hoops

Above their heads

In an effect of extraordinary daring and beauty

Others slowly revolve

Polka dots

Like gambling counters

Artificial palm trees

At the Club New Yorker

Across a tropical island

Set

Covered in yellow clad girls who whirl

Giant bananas

Or turn them

Into a banana xylophone

Carmen Miranda

On top of a wagon

In a hat and corsage

Of bananas and strawberries

Five feet high

With a cornucopia of bananas

Sprouting from her head

As far as the eye can see

A child

JOURNEY TO A STAR

Female flesh

Dissolving into artichokes

Exploding stars

Snowflakes

And the expanding leaves of waterlilies

At the top left hand corner of a dark screen

A Latin American tenor sings

"Brazil"

Moving round the frame

And across a diagonal

Series of bamboo canes

Over

The S.S. Brazil

Arriving in New York Harbor

Passengers bustle down the gangway

Organ grinders' monkeys crawl through

ABSTRACT

To sit posing like a lit host
Beside the wind
Hick snow fur even
Ill blue by green
Drifting hen

THE WATERCOLOR

Way down
up, on
yes no
stop.
Hooray!

The watercolor
is a wonderful
color. Yellow?
Yes. But
beautiful.

What more
there is
is mere
air.
Square air.

THREE HIMALAYAN MINIATURES

Lady caught in a storm,
leaves touching her dress,
snakes and birds—
a storm of love.

*

Girls swimming
in their underpants.
The shoreline
is a graveyard.

*

Lady chasing a cat
that has seized her parrot—
they enter heaven.

LITTLE BLUE HOUSE

Porky the Pig
and Mickey the Mouse
and Donald the Duck
live in my little blue house.

I love you so bad,
you make me so sad,
I think I'll go mad
inside my little blue house.

My animal friends can't help me.
What I need is a picture of your face.
My human friends are taking a vacation
from the human race—

in outer space.

So, Daffy the Duck,
Casper the Ghost
and Elmer the Fudd
live in my little blue house.

I love you so bad,
you make me so sad,
I think I'll go mad
inside my house.

POEM

Screeching NYC
macaws
clothesline to oblivion

Move to Hollywood

get up in the morning
jump into your overalls
chop down your own fruit trees

POEM FOR RICHARD TUTTLE

Zen is then
in French
accent.

SHAVING IN PARIS

Shaving in Paris
Like a millionaire genius
In my window the mirror
Off goes my mustache
Over my shoulder
Students and workers
Shouting in the street
Let us eat cake!
A green scarf
Stuck on the bright yellow wall
In sunlight
Then it rains
We have a *lait grenadine*
In the downstairs cafe
Tripe for lunch
Rain stops we go
Down *Gît-le-Coeur*
1958 beat street
A policemen frowns at the air
A tree is a circle
Tonight we eat at Polidor

POEM (BORN TO BE WILD)

My father said "Listen,
stupid" (he always
called me "Listen")

but I called my father
stupid—he slammed
on the brakes,

teaching me how
to drive
in Germany.

Well known is the long parade of the caterpillars which is brought about by each animal placing its forehead on the ass of the animal in front of it and following. If the lead of the parade falls in a hole out of which it cannot help itself, the parade comes to a stop and is liable to remain at a standstill until all the caterpillars starve. One must guide the lead caterpillar with the help of a decoy which will direct it to the end of the parade, thus placing the lead at the end. Then the parade will proceed in a circle until all marchers perish.

A JUNE CIGARETTE

1. The reflection of the beautician.

2. Walking the pine hills for eternity.

3. Voluntary electrocution by lightning.

DINNER AMERICA

In the street they blow
Mud on your shoe
Scarf cigar
Slam.
Inside
"Bebe" Rebozo to inspect pleasure boats
Then dinner. Dinner America
When a garden grows on the plate
You thought was a mirror
Bong.
Here you reflect on the day's course of events
& wipe your smile away:
Intrigue, malice, paranoia, slander & laughter
Sex, money, divorce, war, dishonesty, violence & scandal—
Little peas & carrots
Flickering in the winter sky

HELLO AGAIN

I like your thin nose
As it appears on this paper.
I like mine, too:
An intelligent and truthful copy.
I liked being with you yesterday.
The ring around the city got pretty blue.
You smoke a lot,
But suddenly and dramatically.
Your wife is terrific.
She is so pretty.
I like the way she drinks her coffee.
Let's get together again real soon.
We're better than anyone else in town.

THE SKELETON

The skeleton has his own
bathing suit

He enjoys swimming and being
in the world

The xylophones are playing
peacefully

The skeleton is dancing
on the beach

We respect his frugality, neatness
patience, tact

He's not just another
skinny person

THE WORLD

The rising steam mingles with the mist
to hide the fig. in the bank
and, at last, the world. The boil murmurs
"See what happens when you're not alive?"

LOVE

Everything is out today
and plausible. Pay attention

to us   humdingers
fading fast   your signal

spring. That you are like
me, a baby bush, confuses

no one, which is they say why
we can work it out   (or else)

Elsie in a field knows why.
The doctor knows.

Let's don't roll on this grass
grass, grass, grass, grass.

It isn't France or even us
a whole tote bag of notions

take wind, memorabilia, the
outstretched arms of the red

and the blue biplanes. Love
in a nervy way, like lightning

nuzzles the chattering tree party
and the sky looks like shantung

to me, and gooey and wavy.

There, there, because you see the way I look, and
in the time you take to tell me, I am changed, then,
now, part imaginary, part yours, a thing, trembling
before another, whose eyes fix me in the shadow and
lose you in the light, or let go, once you are lost,
and in full measure I return the compliment that
gives no pleasure

*

Take you, you're afraid, I could say, there's a
light, going out, now it's night, now it's not,
what I said isn't good, isn't right, I could say,
what I wanted to take couldn't stay, couldn't talk,
stop talking, or wait to be taken away, very slow,
to be awake, you would know, it's not only in these
dreams I can draw a bead on you and hold it there

*

cautious and how you would like to walk beside
yourself, apart from the truth, to see whatever I
could see in you, break the surface of private
water and put off all about you but, how do I look?
and look away, to be loved, and how do you know it's
a lie, you look fine, just fine, a certain way to be
seen, and set apart from me, in the watery distance

*

Always it is uncertain how, standing behind you, it
is with you, how it is now, in a polka dot dress, in
a soft green chair, your arms on its green arms, soft,
the light, I read over your shoulder, breathe down
your neck, now, how to forgive me, wanting desperately
the certainty, you haven't moved from the chair and
the room, sometime in the night

*

SEVEN POEMS

Which way is it you want me to take it, and not
be hurt by your taking pleasure in it, for which,
you stay away from me, a distance, I can't keep,
walking through walls, upstairs and down the hall
to the room where no one can be all there, not
even for the sake of beauty once or twice removed
can I keep this up when I see nothing of either
of us in the dead weight you expect me to carry

*

Time I lost all possible shape, the body cleaved
from desire and returned to a room to be among its
quiet things again, the clock, the lamp, the cabinet,
know their limits, hold back their love or lack of
it, beloved things whose eyes lift to me, weak in
my strength and the reverse, who now may see desire
hovering over the light, the angle and imagination

*

It is only a word my lips won't let go, but the
great one among many that, outside, the heavy air
coming through the branches forces back into me or,
inside, the still air around you forces back into me,
and I think, cruel to yourself, your face asking only
to be left to itself as I plead with myself to speak
and to say it and once and for all, to tell you

terrible shooting pain
in ankle
means
can't work
so no money
soon die

SKY BLUE

The animals enjoy structure
I only understand it
in my house
my face
in the window
a square
blue sky
I'd like to get about
6 ft.
into
but don't.
The "sun" crashes in the "sea".
The human control of purposes is
fantastic.

LANDSCAPE

The little white dog wags his tail
The red mill turns silently
The movie line is a mile long
The sleepyheads toy with their food
The Japanese gardener flies to pieces
Orange soda blows in the wind
A lettuce leaf floats by

DOING

whatever
I feel like
doing

for the rest of my
life
would be nice.

Meanwhile,
there is a
meanwhile.

Where
is
it?

ARKANSAS TRAVELER

You lead a spatial life
In the Ozarks,
Spilling the beans
On your foot,
Which was toeing the mark
Of your rural bliss
Here, only yesterday.
There, only tomorrow
Is another day, Wednesday
Heading your way.
You look left & right—
No sense going anywhere.
A few shrubs
Make a rocking chair.
You rock to & fro—
A boring calm pervades the air.

*

People going up & down,
forward, toward
my eye, by me,
through the town.

*

In the old building
a girl is singing—
when I stop to listen,
she stopped & listened.

*

SONYA'S BEAUTY SALON
What's going on?
Who ever goes there?
No one's ever been there.

*

Poor lady
with a baby
but the baby
doesn't know.

*

An ordinary man is humming
while he works.
He shines my boots and sings—
he shines & hums.

*

NIGGER SUCKS WHITE PRICKS
it says on the subway wall—
I've never heard of such a thing,
but it's funny to think about.

POEMS (1970)

The subway when
no one's there, and then
the train is screaming.
People are screaming.

*

2 nobodies laughing—
bursting—
filling the car.
They became great.

*

A girl in a fur hat
with bulging eyes
rubs against me.
I'm not attracted.

*

I saw a marine,
a U.S. Marine,
in uniform.
That seems unusual.

*

Fat woman in a red dress,
fat woman in a green coat,
in an argument
about lipstick.

IDA LUPINO
for Carla Bley

You look brighter through
the lampshade on my head.

There's a card trick
a cocktail and charades

it's true, Blue Monday
has made monkey man forget.

Pea-green as can be
are you, musically speaking

and walking up & down
on the offbeat in the lobby

a small drunk in brown
toots a blue goodnight:

beige drapes & blinds draw tight.

POEM

Until a few minutes ago
I was catatonic for maybe an hour.
I heard Elisabeth Schwarzkopf sing
Strauss' "September." She sounded drunk.
I thought my wife was dead. I'm stuttering,
Or I think I am when I say something.
I opened the window but don't remember
Opening it, or someone else opened it.
I just called someone to help me.
They're coming down here in a cab.

WOMEN

I'd like to remove one thing
from my sublime life
the awful weakness
of my nervousness.
Nothing satisfies me anymore.
Women know this.

TO MYSELF

Cave,
cave frater,
quia tu credis stare
in alto,
sed caveas de descensu
et quomodo descendis.

Beware,
beware, brother;
you think you are standing
on high,
yet beware of the descent
and whither you will descend.

THE BILL BERKSON STORY

I discovered some bran macaroons, Sunshine,
You can buy in the supermarket, Finast,
But they're Sunshine, which reminds me
Of what Norman Winston said in the Hotel de Paris,
Monte Carlo, at a party given by Elsa (Dinner) Maxwell,
And I sat one person away from Noel Coward (I have a
Photograph). Garbo was there, too, and I was . . . it was
Great. We had this very dog-faced (sad) waiter and
Norman said "Do you have any macaroons?" The waiter
Couldn't believe it. He called for the Maitre D'
Who had a batch macaroons made up special, but it took
1/2 hour (we had coffee). John Gunther was speaking.
Norman built the shopping center where Larry Rivers'
Mural is hanging I think (out at Smithtown) and . . .

WHAT DO PEOPLE DO ALL DAY?

What do people do all day?
Work, cook, make love,
take up time. I pretend
to read or sleep
(red leaves, green branches)
in my impression.
One sun sets in the trees,
another between buildings,
a third in the earth—
a dusty circle.
Insects are in business,
a bee, for instance, zeroes-in
on the hammock. I can see
the air I breathe.
It's one of my hobbies.
People I know
come & go,
those I don't just go.
They have to do something
I can't understand,
pushing themselves into
their outlines, just so
(the bee won't go away)
grinning in the horizon.
It's the end of the day,
they were just fooling around.

A PLAY

1. Man smokes cigarette.

2. Man jacks off.

3. Woman makes breakfast for man.

A voice mounts passionately to the closed mouth,
A wandering voice, like a brazen trumpet or cornet,
A voice that spoke beside me in a bush.
A strenuosity, exquisite, roves in the controlled eye,
A million eyes, a million boots in line,
A civilian passing them by,
A ragged urchin, aimless and alone,
A twelve-year old darling,
A baby with the tail of a rat,
A solitary with a shepherd's smile,
A stranger, named Man,
A stooped man turning out the lights.

A great Huguenot psalm trod forth on the air,
A real classic, though not loud.
A frosty Christmas Eve,
A jostling crowd to laugh and scold at the decree,
A law indifferent to blame or praise,
A new weathervane,
A guileless word, an absurdity,
A senseless order floating in
A world of clear water, brilliant-edged.
A little ship, with oars and food.
A rusty English trawler?
A sea the purple of a peacock's neck,
A surfing party from the isle of task,
A burst of murmurous applause,
A thousand tambourines of glass,
A barrel of salted herrings to last a year.
Hook oo rin you! . . . one herring!
A parting gift from the sea.
A laborer and a factory hand.
A city:—and we have built it, these and I.
A prism over grass-green gorges lone,
A slip of wood I laid,
A part of labor and a part of pain,
A dial with its league-long arm of shade,
A phonograph, a radio, a car and a frigidaire,
A manner of walking, yellow fruit, a house,
A storm of fruit, a mighty cider-reek,
A thousand miles.
A spotted shaft is seen,
A small relation expanding like the shade,
A slippery gumdrop filled with a sweet jelly,
A snow-drop spider, a flower like froth,
A wing's unmoving crumpled end,
A loveless, damned, abortive thing.

A cliff of mighty cowboys,
A mind that would it were
A lion with wings like falling leaves,
A Dante, unprejudiced.
A manifold honey smeared his face,
A more defunctive shroud.
A shudder came over me.
A little sleeping seed, I woke—I did, indeed—
A bruise or break of exit for my life,
A freshness from the inexhaustible vault,
A ripple of the deep-plunged stone of Myth,
A trumpet round the trees. Could one say that it was
A nation of trees, drab green and desolate grey?
A people indistinct as roots of trees?
A host of dry leaves?
A few thousand will think this day
A hardy adventure, full of fear and shock,
A most engrugious notion of the world,
A sacramental relationship,
A flush of rose, and the whole thing starts again.
A peevish bell stammers about the hour of noon.
A cloud comes over the sunlit arch:
A charter to commit the crime once more.
A living man is blind and drinks his drop,
A good old Negro in the slums of the town,
A figure that has grown fabulous,
A long-tailed monster,
A beast with huge antennae and. . . .
A tight arthritic claw.
A little cock is seen,
A horizontal thread.
A foot is shrunk to seven inches,
A live bone sawed! A gentleman! A rondeau!

A clumsy and unrhythmic break . . .
A word torn loose went by me:
A speck that would have been beneath my sight;
A word from which man's grief and wisdom seeps,
A very little thing, a little worm.
A low light is floating through
A few old pecker-fretted apple trees.
A ghostly chord rolls in and grows,
A final clatter of doomed crows seeking
A picture-postcard of June grass.
A spot that pleases me, so charged with waves,
A ship keeps raising its hull.
A door stands open on the evening.
A haunted house. Tenants unknown.
A keen sparkle of frost is on the sill,
A slingshot wide, walled in by towering stone.
A floor too cool for corn,
A shining web, a floating ribbon of cloth,
A faded, pale brownish photograph,
A whisky bottle full of worms,
A somber, sonorous, bitter reservoir,
A guilty panic reason cannot stem,
A burnt beetle like an imitation butler,
A mockery of the ghost in bone,
A throne in darkness, and a power.
A man in a black gown reads from a manuscript.
A poet:
A gaze blank and pitiless as the sun,
A voice as large as fate, a tongue of bronze,
A bantering breed sophistical and swarthy,
A type that will inhabit the dying earth,
A prophet seeking tongues of flame,
A faking builder who stuffs and starches

A POET

A god has power. But can a mere man follow
A beacon, an eternal beam? Flesh fade and mortal trash
A head the color of dust—
A respectable man in his own neighborhood,
A man in his own secret meditation,
A clever boy; and yet appearing to reveal
A lumbering lubbard, loitering slow,
A big, fat, lazy slug,
A way of happening, a mouth,
A tattered coat upon a stick, unless
A serving man that could divine
A sign on high:
A slender tree as vertical as noon,
A mask to try the outer storm of space,
A bleeding eyeless socket, red and dim,
A snowflake of impenetrable cold,
A leopard ranging always in the brow,
A rip-tooth of the sky's acetylene,
A senior soul-flame,
A hollow behind the unbreakable waterfall,
A pond of dusty light.
A little higher?
A gate from earth to non-earth?
A windowpuff-bonnet of fawn-froth,
A missile from that great sling of the past,
A sudden blast of dusty wind,
A hundred inventions ahead of the sky,
A leaping-house of glory,
A huge and birdless silence,
A million atoms drowned in darkness,
A buttress in the air—the void!

FROM THE CHINESE

It was easy to cross the mountains.
It was easy to climb the peaks.
The level roads on the plain turned out to be easiest of all!

STORY BOOK STORY

The roaches jumped stuttering to their feet
The flags fell against the piano
Mr. Sandman entered the iron door
Miss Mouse gave no regard
Listen to me the FBI agents said
But the lunatic shot John Dillinger dead

A WONDERFUL THING
for Ron Padgett

An old farmer and his teenage bride
Are weeping tears of joy
As they ride in their buggy
To a land of peace and plenty.

LITTLE HAND

Tucking up your dress
In the swirling foam
I was on my knees
Your delicious little hand
Queen of pleasure
Weeping like a knife
At the end of life
I loved you so much
That my body become wise
In the bath tub
Again caressed your innocent hand

A LIFE

The baby I thought of
Has hair teeth and eyes
She lives in the little house
Of the mother and dad
Light breezes blow
Rose yellow blue
Rock them along
A line above the sea
They continue along
This way till they die
Then they bring love to heaven

10.

Little picture
stay by me.
Your beautiful face
returns by and by

and you bake pies
and we make love

6.

The day greeting me
is liked by me,
with light, smoke and noise
I rise and float into

7.

You are nude
I am rude
We drink wine
You are mine

8.

I am a jew
You are a jewel
Together we beat
a path to the mule

9.

The earth is ours!
We step on it!
Our women
follow

RHYMES OF A JERK

1.

We are men
We walk like men.
Our women
follow

2.

I am a jew
You are a jewel
Together we beat
a path through the sky!

3.

Tiny maiden
I drink
this beer
to our love

4.

You give me a heart
with your picture.
I pull the string
you go up and down

5.

When the candle dies
we come alive

VALENTINE'S DAY

Reading Tom's poem "To Winter"
weather goes up to 24
though there's no soap
I have a cry in my eye
it's $45 to fly
to a land that's hot & dry
Amsterdam Ave. iced over
Inside Joan sews a purple heart
for John who will read his poem
"Purple Heart" tonight Joan
will wear a purple hat

SMUDGE

You have a little smudge on your forehead, dear,
like a smashed raisin cookie.
I know no reason why I should love you
with my brutal brilliance...
But when you come through that door,
starved, self-righteous,
too solemn for the gaiety of love,
I find your forehead with my mouth
and blow a big raspberry.

SELF-PITY (EAST RIVER)

Somewhere a boat is leaking,
I don't know where.
The sailors may be drowning
but I don't care.
You were away too long
or not long enough.
My clothes don't fit me anymore
but I can see Brooklyn from where I stand
and the building where my clothes were made.
I'd rather be naked in a leafy glade
except for my shoes, playing volleyball
with cheerful pink and ample maids.
But I'll never get out of this world alive.
That was Hank Williams—a bunch of molecules.
I hold my tongue, look across the moon and blink.
You never wrote so you didn't know
a little colored ball of wool was my heart.
12 flights up I light my cigarette,
puff hard and scowl at the river.

*

I get
the idea
I can die
anytime,
then
I forget
it.

*

When a tree falls
on your head
it says yes
or no.

*

I walk
you walk
we walk

through
each
other

into
our
selves

*

The evil eye
is ridiculous
but it exists.

*

PERSONAL

I'd like
to keep
myself

out
of this...
this...

whatever
you
call it.

*

It's too easy
to say
yes,
now—

difficult
to think,
say,
now.

I whistle
softly
to myself.

*

a red
tin pan
of tan
doom

*

Gravity
pulls
me
down

so
hard
I
can

only
say
my
name.

*

"When my head
goes too fast
I get out
and walk."

TWELVE POEMS

A balloon
is going up
filled with problems.

*

SELF

In my pale
face
is a grim

mask,
but I have
to laugh.

My arm
is a bone—
I

love
it
so.

*

When I think
of the thought
machines

FOR JENNIFER

Electric pencil sharpener
Paper, paints
House maples
Eyes are no eyes
Friends are faces
Stuck to feelings
Sleeping on the beach
Patience for changes to make
Take effect
Work, laughter
Shopping eating
There are some problems for help
It's like a bake sale
People, books
Circle in a wheel
Gray for sky
Green for leaves

7

O wandering poet
Often loitering on your path
Letting your hair float
In the superhuman ether
It is the time for jealous tenderness
Smiles flowers kisses perfume happiness
Wafted in the night wind
After insipid poetry reading
Light up your fantasy
Strew the ideal path with lingering glances
Lilies lips and sandal-wood!
O fantasy of Betty Codell!

8

Rings of Anselm
Numbering the colors
As secrets ride by
In panels of sunlight
The walls bounce
Squares and hearts
On the speckled eyelids
Of the dreaming typist

4

Mankind is returning to barbarism
Men's eyes like furnace doors ajar
There are no crosses in the quarters of the compass
We learn in the dark the darkness in us

5

I used to work in Chicago
In a department store
Went to kindergarten, too
Girlbaby classmate
Vanished
Later found
All over town
Cops & volunteers
Picked up packaged pieces
Different departments
We split town

6

I remember pumpkins
Battle Creek
"White Christmas"
For 2000 GI's
I sang wobbly
Got a big hand
Flushed
Dapper little jewboy
1942

TAP ROOTS

for Ted & Alice

1

Such pure moon-white waxen blossoms
On the sidewalk
I sit drinking and do not notice the dusk
Till falling petals fill the folds of my jacket

2

O barren Wrigley Field, bleak with chilly air,
Forbidding pasturage or the ploughman's care,
Saffron poles a beauteous bloom disclose,
And chalk foul lines a gloomy grove compose.

3

The blue dreamlight is full of beetles
The apple's transparent flesh will feed the chickens
Lovers Leap is filled with oaks and silver poplars
Dr Foster in the moonlight as agile as a gymnast
Ah forwards and backwards he'll confuse the werewolf
    pigfuckers
Then comes a woman with a short stick
"The toes on your feet are much to be appreciated"
Earth is low tightening dull revolutions of treetops
Vapor trails diffusing fragile networks of old tortoise
    shells

NICE DOGGY

Most beautiful day
For modes of thought
To fly around and eat fried chicken

But a waitress cloud bosom
Hovers near in the blue
Over the town's longest lawn

Nice doggy
Lift your leg

Then he rounds the corner
Conditioning the future
Beyond itself

AT THE OFFICE

Some women are in the room so I go
Through to the other side
White sun rolls out on top of the air
I can't understand the space of the cars
Returning to the office I notice women leaving
I opened the door and was sprayed with hot water

CONSCIOUS

1

Who is that? Eduardo Cianelli? George Coulouris? Victor Francen? George Zucco? Berry Kroeger? Huh? Abner Biberman? Paul Cavanaugh? Charles Dingle? Harold Huber? Help! Cy Kendall? Ian MacDonald? Who's there???

2

Stacked, slow-motion clips of javelin throwers at the lunging instant of release, and more stacked clips of the quivering shafts jabbing the turf.

3

Seven sweaty, shimmering Finns, naked, genitals revealed, luxuriate in their sauna.

4

Rubber bag filled with feathers.

Slip-on erasers. It completely covered the sharp
Point of the rod and protected the fresh, frail curtains
As I drew them onto the rods. Saved the curtains and
Saved time, too. Tom and I, inveterate coffee drinkers,
Recently acquired a new glass electric percolator that
Immediately became our favorite. It perks the coffee
Slowly and evenly (which certainly affects the flavor),
Has five strength settings, makes up to ten cups, and is,
Of course, automatic. Cotton swabs, by the way, have
Many uses at our house.

Why don't you put Sunbrella awnings on your house?

BIG MESS

for Kenward Elmslie

An antique wicker settee, cousin of the "meridiennes"
The Empress Eugenie made fashionable (she used them
For after-lunch naps), sits with enormous panache
In an otherwise calm and contemporary room in a house
On a hill, having certain advantages that its valley
Neighbors can seldom rival, once the problems implicit
In building on a slope have been solved. We have
A friend who is famous for her onion soup and we love
To gather at her house informally, for onion soup,
Wonderful breads and cheeses, fruit, and interesting
Coffee. I have begun to pick up pretty bits for
Summer entertaining whenever I see them. Found some
Delightful trivets and coasters at Bonwit Teller
The day I was in Philadelphia—large slices of water-
Melon, orange, pink grapefruit, lemon and lime made of
Sparkling Lucite, in more or less life sizes and colors.
What could be nicer for our glass-topped table? Windows,
Which seem to slumber all winter as part of the wall,
Take on a renewed importance with the arrival of early
Spring. Even before we open them wide to the world
We are drawn to the garden and gawk at the sky. Taking
My cue from a fine late-April day I had all the windows
Washed, sent some curtains to be cleaned, and laundered
The washable ones myself. First I did the scalloped
Organdy curtains in our bedroom—easy enough. But when
I went to slip them back on their brass rods I was
Worried about tearing them, till I hit on a good idea.
Before attempting to slide each rod through the curtain
Hem, I placed over the end of it one of those tapered

THEM AGAIN

And me
In eskimo land
Tearing them to pieces
Less and less
Nude with cat
I carried the stairs up you
And using them they will not appear used
But much plainer
In the stuffed chair of the north wing
While the characteristics of the landscape
Before the landscape is discovered settle
It's the middle of the day
I'm wearing an ordinary pair of house slippers

TWO DREAM POEMS

Soft white curtains
leave the window
believe the window
I'd

   like to dedicate this
meaning

*

The drummer
& drum

    the feeling everything
let go

The end.

The meeting a friend
              a looseness

AN IDEAL LIFE

When the sun shines
I'm up with the birds
orange blue red green

bath breakfast walk
across the city
visit and talk

with P, C, M & E
home again write
rest and read

A light lunch
letters to D
K, F, R & T

records and the radio
a substantial dinner
go to a show

Back home exercise
smoke some dope
close my eyes

THE SHADOW

Like a mammoth black pall came the onrushing shadow. The large white cloud grew grey, then dark as the shadow raced toward the plane. The shadow bands danced their fantastic movements on the white t-shirts of those near at hand. The mighty shadow enveloped the racing plane. Hazes and thin clouds of the sky above caught the crepelike shadow. Then, as suddenly as it came, the shadow was gone.

THE GOD

Up here the image of the world
makes itself true.
At times a thing comes secretly
to stand beside him when he's squeezing

the image down there
neither inside nor out
squandering his estate
on that image he forgets but

he keeps on pushing
his face up to it.
Almost but not quite
then stopping: he can't *be*.

IN A LOUD RESTAURANT

We sat in a loud restaurant and made more noise than everyone, forgiving one another nothing. In lower tones we said it wasn't fair to torture each other. Then we fell silent and ate a huge meal. I was thinking what I would do about finding a new place to stay and what I would do with all my books and records when, all of a sudden, in the loud restaurant mirror, I saw, in the light flashing in the short hairs on the back of your neck, a perfectly clear photograph of Our Lord.

A STICK FIGURE

Your indestructible body
Is your mind's present
Image of itself—you're fine.
You make me laugh and snap
My head back till it aches.
Your spider legs
Do the mashed potato,
The monkey.
Tufts of your hair
Flutter in the air.

VALENTINE

Silly
little
underhanded
rabbit,

shiny red heart
racing
over your bedroom
floor.

BIRDS

Grey birds
with red stripes
fly straight

at me,
framed by
2 sky-

scrapers.
I lie
in bed

with a
sick
leg.

STILL LIFE

The lamp over the table
on heavy iron chain
slippers underneath
AQUABEE
bright light on a fly
near a penny
I'm in my shoes
Here's looking at you
& here isn't
Your new tv
watches me
take a drink
You go I drink
Sammy Davis, Jr
says he's sorry
in hospital corridor
Miami, Florida

THINGS

I
feel
an
ache
of
anxiety
because
this
person
toward
whom
I
feel
kindly
is
a
crazy
person
and
I
could
make
her
crazier
(more
crazy)
if
I
said
the
wrong
things.

BRAIN DAMAGE

Feeling like I had been droped from bulding
I stagered from the car nut reall hurt jus shok op
and before I knew it I was crasy.

I seem to ho a pij wit the force ova rikjet
Prof bentley the vibrati incres seem to be arub.
Others tracked it too probebly.

JEEPERS Pete l-lokk at dot cresy   Hay!!!
is the bih vtrrrp we been hearin about?
HAVE YOU GONE bats

No no I let you fire at it you are rong
look at it!

I bombardded the ho

THE JOKE

My wife was a joke
I told a man
who slept with her
the night before.

Had she heard
the cost
would have been
no love lost.

One night in bed
the joke
lit a cigarette
and blew smoke

in my face
which is no disgrace.
Now she and her lover
are free of each other

and he sits in a chair
and laughs at her
and makes an obscene gesture
in the air.

ONE DAY IN NOVEMBER

One day in November an
Indian chief with a prominent erection
Came to tea. He sat erect in his chair
Holding the erection in front of his chest.
It never moved but we knew he was ill at ease.

In bed, and had a nice cup of hot cocoa
With a few chocolate-chip cookies. Then I
Turned out the light and had this terrible dream.

OCCASIONAL POEM

Tom Clark and I went out to Greenwich
And spread our lunch on Greenwich Green.
There were ham and cheese sandwiches, peanut
Butter and jelly sandwiches, 1/2 lb. potato
Salad, sweet and sour pickles, two cans
Of black cherry soda, and some crumb cake
My mother baked. After lunch and cigarettes
We played catch with a red rubber ball, which
Neither of us dropped, on Greenwich Green.
It was a splendid day! The hot sun was killing
All the germs on everybody's face, and kids
And their nannies raced around like nobody's
Business. Then, Tom and I went off to see
The Queen's House and, in the Maritime
Museum, under a microscope, the smallest
Cannon in the world. We wondered how
They ever managed to put it together. Yeah.

Toward the end of the day we went to have
A coke in a small cafe nearby. Tom seemed
Depressed so I told a joke to cheer him up.
(Earlier, I had complained of one of my
Famous stomach aches. Go to the bathroom,
Tom suggested. I did and felt lots better.)
The sun was going down. We took a bus to town.
Tom caught his train and I, I caught mine.

When I got home I ate a good turkey dinner
With blueberry pie a la mode for dessert.
I watched a little TV, read for a while

VOTS

The flowers smile
showing their gums
You walk around
them in shiny boots
to where I am munching
a duck salami sandwich
pale orange light
on library lawn
You smile
banging your mouth shut
I read
new Brautigan book
An old green bum
drinking Ballerina Vodka
can't tie his shoe
begins to cry softly
fucking shoe
blows his nose
in the *Chronicle*
We go off to see
Anna Christie
Garbo says
vots der use

NEW YORK

The radiator came on & the geraniums died.
Finally throwing up all the arms on the page,
They came down in bangs, spilling mucilage
& some ink. Someone. I was careful to move
                                      a muscle . . .
I thought I witnessed an assist
From it. In &/or Out of the Blue. Not
A cloud. A huge network of dots got
Connected, would prove ghostly.
Nor swan nor clown, but machinery
For lowering or raising heavenly objects.
When I rushed to pull the shade, the sky-
Writers wrote Yanks 5, Reds 3,
Across the page & would-be face. Then my ears
Burned & I cheered, remembering what name
                                      & team

Story Book Story	43
From the Chinese	44
A Poet	45
A Play	50
What Do People Do All Day?	51
The Bill Berkson Story	52
To Myself	53
Women	54
Poem	55
Ida Lupino	56
Poems (1970)	57
Arkansas Traveler	60
Doing	61
Landscape	62
Sky Blue	63
Terrible Shooting Pain	64
Seven Poems	65
Love	68
The World	69
Skeleton	70
Hello Again	71
Dinner America	72
A June Cigarette	73
Well known is the long parade of caterpillars	74
Poem (Born to be Wild)	75
Shaving in Paris	76
Poem for Richard Tuttle	77
Poem	78
Little Blue House	79
Three Himalayan Miniatures	80
The Watercolor	81
Abstract	82
Journey to a Star	83
Last Poem	88

CONTENTS

New York	3
Vots	4
Occasional Poem	5
One Day in November	7
The Joke	8
Brain Damage	9
Things	10
Still Life	11
Birds	12
Valentine	13
A Stick Figure	14
In a Loud Restaurant	15
The God	16
The Shadow	17
An Ideal Life	18
Two Dream Poems	19
Them Again	20
Big Mess	21
Conscious	23
At the Office	24
Nice Doggy	25
Tap Roots	26
For Jennifer	29
Twelve Poems	30
Self-Pity (East River)	34
Smudge	35
Valentine's Day	36
Rhymes of a Jerk	37
A Life	40
Little Hand	41
A Wonderful Thing	42

For Joan

Some of these poems were published in the following magazines and anthologies: *Acid, Angel Hair, Another World, Azu, Best & Company, Big Sky, 'C', The (Chicago) Seed, Frice, Occulist Witnesses, Out There, The Paris Review, Sesheta, Strange Faeces, The World, The World Anthology, Yale Literary Magazine.* "A Poet" was written in collaboration with Clark Coolidge.

Copyright © Larry Fagin 1978

Library of Congress Cataloging in Publication Data

Fagin, Larry.
   I'll be seeing you.
   I. Title
PS3556.A3314   811'.5'4   77-28219

ISBN 0-916190-10-2
ISBN 0-916190-11-0 pbk.

First edition

I'LL BE SEEING YOU
Poems 1962-1976

Larry Fagin

Full Court Press